Builder Brothers
BIG PLANS

No dreamer is ever too small; no dream is ever too big. This book is for all the clever, creative kids out there. You can and will do anything you set your mind to!

—Drew and Jonathan Scott

ISBN 978-0-06-284662-4 (trade bdg.) — ISBN 978-0-06-287046-9 (special edition)
— ISBN 978-0-06-288921-8 (special edition)

by Drew and Jonathan Scott
The artist used Adobe Photoshop to create the illustrations for this book.
Typography by Rick Farley
18 19 20 21 22 PC 10 9 8 7 6 5 4 3 2 1

❖
First Edition

Builder Brothers
BIG PLANS

Drew and Jonathan Scott

Illustrated by Kim Smith

HARPER

An Imprint of HarperCollinsPublishers

One sweet summer afternoon, Drew and Jonathan
were doing what they did best: dreaming big.

"Let's build a tree house," said Drew.

"No, a castle," said Jonathan.

"With a firefighter's pole!"

"And a catapult!"

The twins were always making big plans. But for some reason, grown-ups only ever laughed.

"That sounds like quite a creative castle that you boys are going to build." Uncle Joe chuckled. "Hmmm," said Aunt Cathy. "Sounds like your imagination might be a little too wild."

The twins shuffled off to their official planning table (a.k.a. the dining table).

"They never think we can *actually* build these things," said Jonathan.

"Just because we're little," said Drew.

"But little people can do big things."
The brothers traded a grin. "We'll show them!"

But how?

They rummaged and rooted through their plans. They paced and pondered. They buckled down and brainstormed.

This project had to be absolutely perfect, but absolutely nothing they came up with felt quite right.

"Feels like the perfect idea is right in front of our noses," said Jonathan.

"Yup," said Drew.

And that's when they noticed . . .

Gracie
and
Stewie!

"Are you thinking what I'm thinking?" asked Drew.

"Even before you think it," said Jonathan. "Let's build . . ."

"A double-decker doghouse!" cried the brothers.

In a flash, the boys grabbed paper and pencils and started working.
They sketched and scribbled, doodled and designed, colored and created.

And when they were done, they stepped back to look at the result and said together, "This will be the most awesomest double-decker doghouse ever!"

They pooled all their savings.

And they plunked down their plans, their shopping list, and all their money on the counter.

"We want to build the most awesomest double-decker doghouse ever!" said Drew.

The store worker pored over their plans. She read their list up and down. "You boys sure this is *all* you want?" she asked. "It seems kind of small."

"Sure, we're sure," said Drew.

"Nobody thinks we can," said Jonathan.

"But little people can do big things!"

The brothers were so excited that they raced each other all the way home.

Drew and Jonathan hurried into their garage.
For the next few hours, all you could hear was . . .

At last, the brothers stepped back to admire their work. The double-decker doghouse was awesome, all right, but it was also . . .

GRACIE

STEWIE

. . . WAY too small!

"Oops," said Drew.

"Uh-oh," said Jonathan. "I think we must have measured wrong."

"What now?" said Drew.

The brothers flopped down on the floor. Were the grown-ups right after all? Their money was gone, their work was done, and the twins had nothing to show for it.

How could Drew and Jonathan turn their teeny-tiny doghouse into something worthy of all that work?

The brothers looked up. Then their eyes met.

"Are you thinking what I'm thinking?" asked Jonathan.

"Even before you think it," said Drew.

And with a bit more tinkering, toying, and tuning up, the brothers turned their tiny doghouse into a super-duper deluxe birdhouse!

That night, as they crawled into their beds, Jonathan said, "I bet those birds are dreaming their own big dreams in their new house right now."

Drew asked, "But where will Gracie and Stewie sleep?"

At first, Jonathan wondered.

But then he realized the dogs didn't need a house. They were already right where they belonged.

As they slipped off to sleep, the brothers smiled. Because they knew what every builder knows: every big plan starts with a dream.

Build your own birdhouse!

You can build a birdhouse too, with just a little help from a grown-up.
Important: Do not do this activity without adult supervision.

Here's what you need:

- [ ] One empty half-gallon milk or juice cardboard carton, cleaned and dried
- [ ] Construction paper in various colors
- [ ] Scissors
- [ ] Rubber cement
- [ ] Markers and/or crayons
- [ ] Craft knife
- [ ] A long twig
- [ ] String

Instructions:

Step 1. Cover each side of the carton with construction paper. Get a grown-up to help you measure and cut the paper.

Step 2. Glue each panel onto the carton. Decorate the paper with images from magazines or drawings.

Step 3. With a grown-up's help, use a craft knife to cut a 2" x 2" square on one side of the carton, about 2" from the bottom.

Step 4. Poke two holes in the carton, one an inch below the open square, and one on the opposite side. Stick the twig through these holes so your birds can perch on it.

Step 5. Poke a hole in the top of the carton, then tie a loop of string through the hole so you can hang the birdhouse up.

Extra Fun: Use spray primer instead of construction paper to coat the carton. Then you'll have a blank surface to color. Spray the primer, let it dry, and then decorate it however you like. Spray it with safe, clear sealant to make it weather resistant! Just make sure you have an adult's supervision throughout the process.